LITTLE CHANGES

Acknowledgements

My heartfelt thanks go out to all those who contributed to this project and helped me turn ideas into scribbles, scribbles into poetry, and poetry into this book.
I hope that you will learn from, pass on, but mostly enjoy this story.

My endless gratitude goes to the European Society of Evolutionary Biology for funding, James Munro for the beautiful illustrations, Paul Taylor of Inner Planet for the snazzy website, Nicola Ibberson for donating half of her hard earned prize money from I'm a Scientist, Get me out of Here! to the cause, and a long list of critical readers who gave priceless advice and guidance including Ailsa Stevens, Ellie Decamp, Christopher Jones, Britt Koskella, Louise Johnson and Deni Price.

LITTLE CHANGES

by Tiffany Taylor

Illustrations by James Munro

Once a long, long time ago, and even longer still,
Past your school, down the road, and far beyond the hill,
Over the sea, and frozen mountains, with their snow-capped heads,
Through the darkest forest, past the dried-up riverbed,

There lived a troop, or so they say, of old forgotten creatures,
Different in their manners and more bizarre in their features,
Sweet enough in nature, and smart enough in mind,
They were called the rinkidinks, the last ones of their kind.

They lived together in the forest hidden by the trees,

Little beasts that wouldn't come much taller than your knees,

Round of face, and round of belly, camouflaged in green,

With long, strong tails that flicked behind,

the strangest things you've seen!

As much as they all looked the same, up close each was unique,

With slightly different faces and different in physique.

Different markings, different heights, different eyes to see,

All the same, but each one special, just like you and me.

The rinkidinks were carefree sorts, and every day was fine,

They'd eat and sleep for all the day, and play to pass the time.

And when they were feeling hungry some would go and see

If they could find their favourite fruits, high up in the trees.

The grubblegob was for some the tastiest kind of treat;

Juicy and delicious, they were the finest fruits to eat.

Pink and yellow berries, and purple spotty leaves,

But the only place to find them was at the tippy tops of trees.

But how could they get up there without the use of wings?

A few of them had the skill to use their tails as springs!

They'd coil them tight, and with a leap, fly up into the trees,

And all would cheer as they would bounce with such apparent ease.

But others of the rinkidinks liked a different fruit instead,

That, far from growing up in trees grew down on the riverbed!

The runglesnip was big and dull, with a tough and hardy skin;

But look inside and you would find scrumptiousness within.

Some courageous rinkidinks could use their tails to swim,

The others watched, while effortlessly they would dive straight in.

They'd fill their cheeks till fit to burst with runglesnips galore,

Then eat, and eat until they could not possibly eat more.

The rinkidinks were carefree sorts, as I have said before,

So how could they anticipate what there could be in store?

One rainy day the river swelled and burst out at the bank,

And the rinkidinks could only watch as all they knew was sank.

Some of them, they ran for cover, up to higher grounds,

And of those with springy tails they jumped in leaps and bounds,

And found themselves on drier land and each of them was pleased,

When they looked up to grubblegobs, hanging from the trees.

Others taken by the flood, they used their tails to swim,

For miles they were carried on, as more water came in,

But soon enough the waters calmed, and it was then they saw

Beneath their feet, more runglesnips than they'd ever seen before.

Those high up on the hillside found the only way to feed,

Was using tails to spring up to the grubblegobs they'd need,

But those washed down to the valley, couldn't reach up high,

So using tails they'd swim to runglesnips to get them by.

Now far apart these rinkidinks they had to start again,

As two new groups, and overtime slowly settle in.

But soon enough this foreign place, began to feel like home,

And so they grew, and made new nests for families of their own.

You may not know, so I'll explain, about the rinkidink;

To raise a baby is, I've heard, much harder than you think!

They cry and moan, they scream and sulk, they squabble and they fight,

And more monstrous than their temper tantrums are their appetites!

The parents must work really hard to find the food they need,

And a bigger family means more little mouths to feed.

So those who have the special tails (best for fetching fruit)

Can have more baby rinkidinks: messy, exhausting, but cute.

Have you ever noticed when you look at families

That they all look a bit alike, sharing similarities?

Nose and ears, teeth and smile, hair colour and eyes,

And that's because they're all made from the same stuff inside.

The rinkidinks are just the same, and it's easy to see

Which little baby rinkidink comes from which family.

But important for this story is one feature that they share:

A tail much like their mum and dad on their furry derrière.

As years raced by, those on the hill spent less time on the ground,

And so it was that other things could help them get around,

Long arms helped them sway and swing between the slender branches,

So they could reach the tastiest fruit, without taking any chances.

Whereas in the valley large paws helped them swim,

And a dense and downy fur meant no water could get in!

So in the end, and given time, these strange peculiar creatures,

Once so alike in all they were now shared different features.

Until one day, whilst wandering, two strangers they caught sight,

One was short and tubby; the other tall and slight,

So different in so many ways: their tail, their shape, their skin;

That how could they imagine, that their ancestors were kin?

But trace the families far enough, and travel back in time,

Following their history in a long unbroken line,

Focus on their differences and you never would have guessed,

That their great great great great great
    great great great great great
      great great great great
       great great great
       great great
       great
       great
       great
      great…
grandparents, shared a family nest.

But the story of the rinkidinks is not a special one at all,

For anything that's ever lived has done it all before.

And every plant or animal from mountain, sea, or plain,

Has a lengthy family history, which is in many ways the same.

Life is in itself a challenge which everything must face,

And the skills you need to stay alive will change from place to place.

But within each group or family there is a way to a solution,

And it's the ability to best the rest, which we call evolution.

I wonder if you can think of something, maybe at the zoo,

That seems perfectly shaped for all the things that it might do.

Necks to stretch, teeth to bite, or big round brains to think,

And imagine the story behind it all, just like the rinkidink.